Search and *and* SP⊙T

Go!

Laura Ljungkvist

Houghton Mifflin Harcourt

Boston   New York

Let's Go!

There are so many ways
to travel and so many places to visit.
You can go by land, air, or sea—
but just GO!

SEARCH and SPOT

6 green things you would pedal,

5 blue things you would sail,

and 7 pink things you would fly.

If you go by car, it is sometimes tricky to find where you left it in a big parking lot. Turn the page and

SEARCH *and* **SPOT**

these cars, as well as

7 cars with a missing tire,

8 convertibles with their tops down,

9 cars parked the opposite way,

and 1 old taxicab.

If you can't drive,
why not go on a bike?

SEARCH *and* **SPOT**

7 bicycles colored the same as the one below,

3 bikes that are pink and blue,

3 that are black and green,

and 1 that is black and orange.

Getting tired on your bicycle?
Motorbikes go much faster and
you don't have to pedal!

SEARCH *and* **SPOT**

all the motorbikes you see below,

5 motorbikes with flat tires,

2 with 4 lights,

and 1 that lost its saddle.

Going by bus is a great way
to get around your city or town.
But it's important to hop on
the right one!

SEARCH *and* **SPOT**

bus M83,

6 buses that are out of service,

and 1 that doesn't know

where it is going.

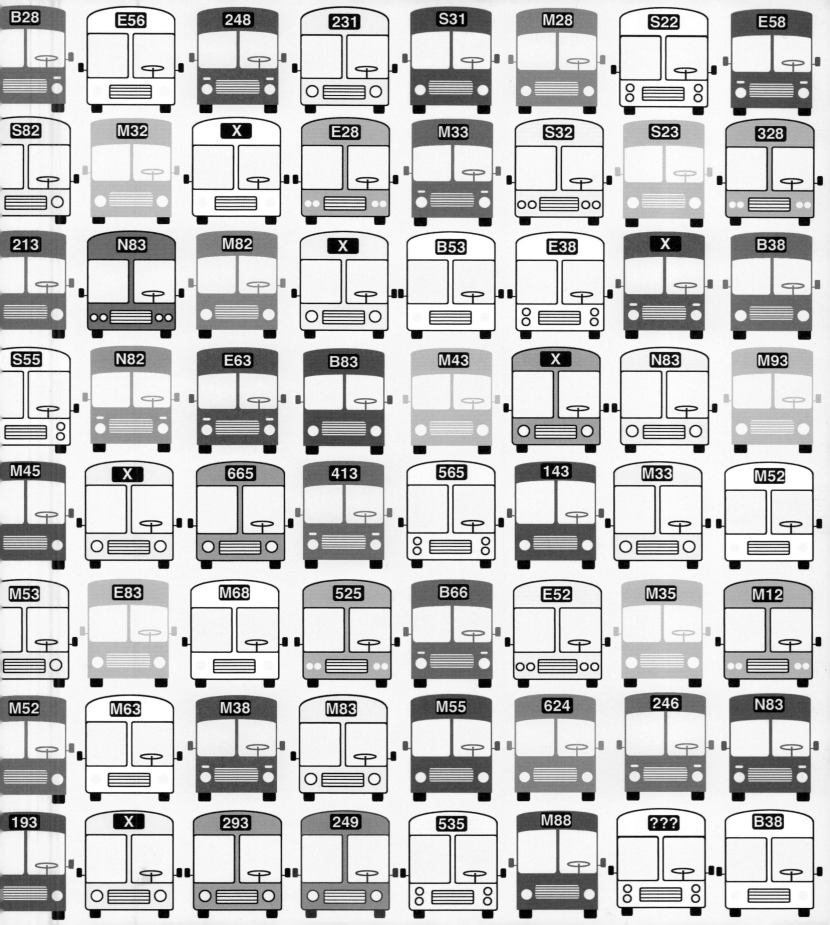

Some vehicles
have important jobs.
When they go, they go to work.

SEARCH *and* **SPOT**

all the vehicles you see below,

4 blue boxes being picked up,

and 1 truck delivering

a big present.

There are other vehicles
that have **very** important jobs.
They help save lives in emergencies!

SEARCH *and* **SPOT**

the ambulances below,

7 helicopters,

4 fire engines,

and 1 police car.

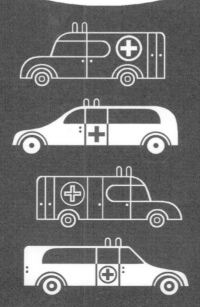

With so many
vehicles driving on the roads,
traffic signs show them **how** to go.
Turn the page, and

SEARCH *and* **SPOT**

all of these helpful signs,

6 round signs that have bicycles on them,

7 signs with buses,

6 that say STOP,

and 3 musical signs.

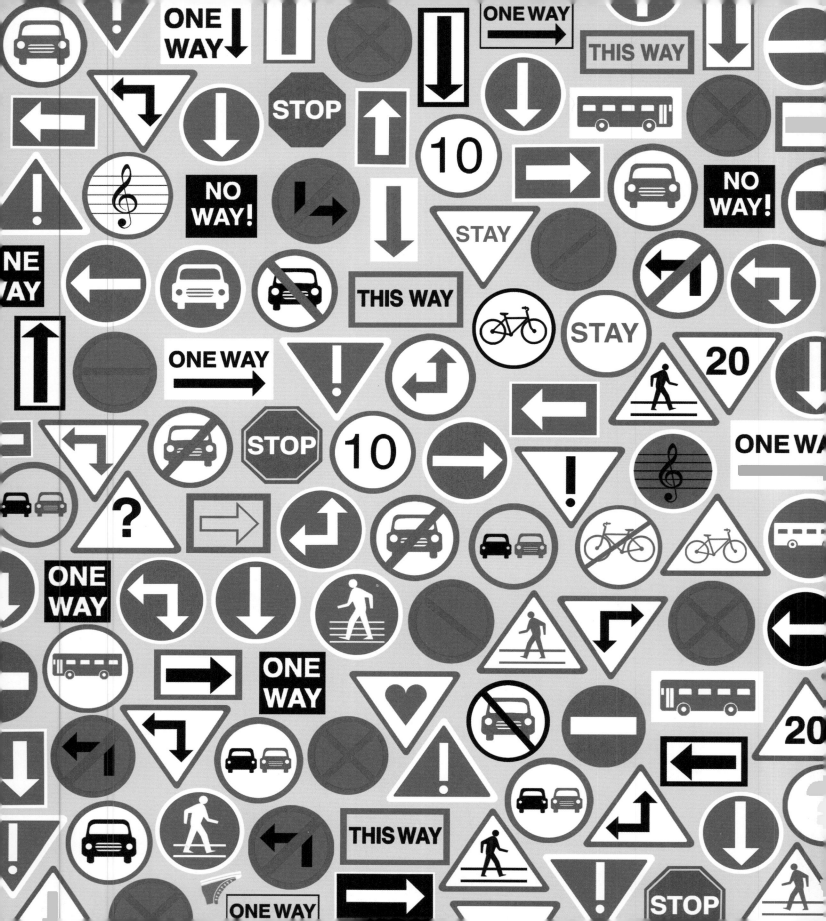

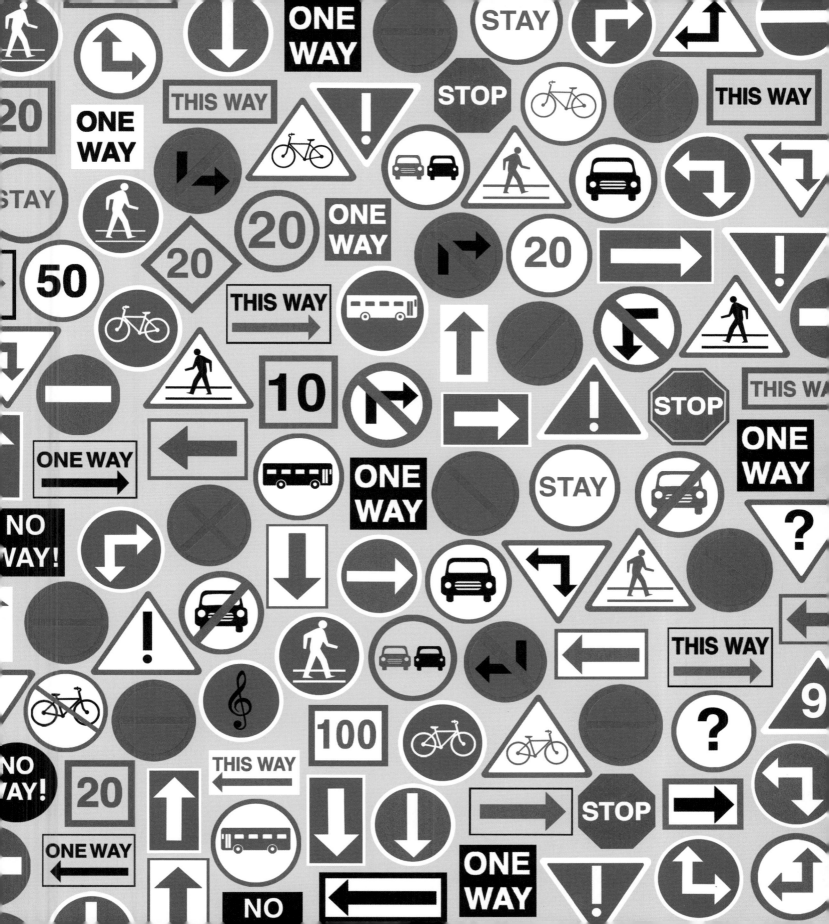

If you get lost,
there are maps to show
you **where** to go!

SEARCH *and* **SPOT**

1 church,

2 parking lots,

1 flower garden,

1 hospital,

and 1 dog run.

Starting here, see if you can find
your way to all of these places.

Lots of vessels go
on the ocean, lakes, and rivers.
Turn the page, and

SEARCH *and* **SPOT**

all of these boats and ships,

13 anchors,

4 fishing boats,

and 1 submarine.

Many things that go
fly high in the air.

SEARCH *and* **SPOT**

10 helicopters,

10 hot air balloons,

8 airplanes with one propeller,

and 6 planes that have 2 propellers.

When night comes,
it's time to go home.

SEARCH *and* **SPOT**

a car, a bike, and a motorcycle
that don't have any lights on,
2 ambulances with the sirens on,
and 1 small kitten trying to
find its way home.

After exploring
all these different ways to go,
let's **walk** home! All you
need are shoes!

SEARCH *and* SPOT

for these four sneakers that were lost

somewhere along the way.

P&V, always and forever. —L.L.

The text of this book is set in Tw Cen MT and Rockwell. The illustrations are created digitally.

ISBN: 978-0-544-57042-9 | Manufactured in China | SCP 10 9 8 7 6 5 4 3 2 1 | 4500601193

Need help finding anything?
Go to **WWW.HMHBOOKS.COM/SEARCHANDSPOT**